CLASSIC STARTS™

Great Expectations

Retold from the Charles Dickens original
by Deanna McFadden

Illustrated by Eric Freeberg

STERLING

New York / London
www.sterlingpublishing.com/kids

STERLING and the distinctive Sterling logo
are registered trademarks of Sterling Publishing Co., Inc.

Library of Congress Cataloging-in-Publication Data

McFadden, Deanna.
  Great expectations / retold from the Charles Dickens original by
Deanna McFadden ; illustrated by Eric Freeberg.
      p. cm. — (Classic starts)
  Summary: The adventures of an orphaned young man in Victorian England
who is given a great deal of money by an unknown benefactor to enable him to
live as a gentleman, pursuing a good education and fulfilling great expectations.
  ISBN 978-1-4027-6645-9
  [1. Orphans—Fiction. 2. Coming of age—Fiction. 3. Great Britain—History—
19th century—Fiction.] I. Freeberg, Eric, ill. II. Dickens, Charles, 1812–1870.
Great expectations. III. Title.
  PZ7.M4784548Gr 2010
  [Fic]—dc22

                                                                        2009013956

Lot#:
2 4 6 8 10 9 7 5 3 1
11/09
Published by Sterling Publishing Co., Inc.
387 Park Avenue South, New York, NY 10016
Text © 2010 by Deanna McFadden
Illustrations © 2010 by Eric Freeberg
Distributed in Canada by Sterling Publishing
^c/o Canadian Manda Group, 165 Dufferin Street
Toronto, Ontario, Canada M6K 3H6
Distributed in the United Kingdom by GMC Distribution Services
Castle Place, 166 High Street, Lewes, East Sussex, England BN7 1XU
Distributed in Australia by Capricorn Link (Australia) Pty. Ltd.
P.O. Box 704, Windsor, NSW 2756, Australia

Classic Starts is a trademark of Sterling Publishing Co., Inc.

Sterling ISBN 978-1-4027-6645-9

For information about custom editions, special sales, premium and
corporate purchases, please contact Sterling Special Sales
Department at 800-805-5489 or specialsales@sterlingpublishing.com.

CONTENTS

CHAPTER 1

Christmas Eve

I was born Philip Pirrip. As a little boy, I found it hard to say my name. So I became Pip, and I've been called that ever since. My mother, father, and five brothers all died when I was very young. On a day like today, when I'm sitting by their tombstones, I imagine my mother with freckles and my father with curly black hair. Being an orphan would have been worse had I not lived with my sister, Mrs. Joe Gargery. She was twenty years older than me and married to a blacksmith. Our house was next to the forge, where Joe kept

Joe kept a great fire going to work with his metal at any time of day.

It was Christmas Eve. A cold breeze rushed over the marsh, and the sea crashed in the distance. My teeth chattered. My body shivered. I missed my parents. Alone by their graves in the churchyard, the sounds of the wind and water scared me. I sat down and started to cry.

"Be quiet!" a man shouted. "Stay still or you'll be sorry."

I looked up to find a scary-looking man. He wore rough gray pants and an old rag for a hat. A giant prison cuff was wrapped around his leg. Wet, muddy, and limping, he glared at me.

"P-p-please don't hurt me," I begged.

"What's your name? Quickly!"

"Pip."

"Point to where you live!"

I had just lifted my arm when suddenly the world was upside down! The man had me by the heels and shook me hard. A piece of bread dropped to the ground from my pocket. Moments later the church was right-side up again.

"Where are your parents?" He licked his lips.

"There and there." I tipped my head to either side as I held tight to a tombstone.

"Who do you live with if your parents are buried here?" He stepped forward, grabbed me by the shoulders, and tilted me backward.

"My sister, sir, and her husband, the blacksmith, Joe Gargery."

A glint came into his eye. "The next question is whether or not I'm going to *hurt* you." His fingers gripped my arms tightly. "You know what a file is, right?"

I nodded.

"And you know what food is, *right?*"

I nodded again.

"You're going to get me a file, and you're going

to get me some food. You'll bring them both to me at the old shipyard tomorrow morning—or *else*." He released me from his grip. "You'll remember every bit of this conversation, right?"

"Y-yes, sir."

"Good," he said as he walked away. "Now get going."

Too afraid to move, I watched as he limped toward the church wall. Just before he crawled over, he looked back. One glance from him sent me running home as fast as I could.

Joe was sitting alone in the kitchen when I returned, his blacksmith shop closed for the night. He said, as sweet and as calm as ever, "Your sister's out looking for you. She's been and gone a dozen times and worked up a temper."

My sister burst into the room then, screaming, "Where have you been, you rascal?"

I said, "The churchyard."

"I walked by there twice and I didn't see

you!" She didn't wait for an answer. "You might as well have stayed there for all the time I've wasted looking for you! Sit in the corner while I make dinner."

My stomach growled with hunger, but I didn't dare eat the slice of bread she gave me for dinner. I had to save food for the man. When my sister wasn't looking, I quickly put the bread down my pant leg. When Joe saw it was gone, he made a face. My sister said, "What on earth is the matter now? Why do you look so funny?"

"You can't have chewed that bread, Pip," Joe said.

"Have you been eating too fast again?" She pulled me up by the ear. "Sure as I have two feet your stomach will ache. You're taking some medicine."

A spoon was forced into my mouth. I swallowed the foul mixture. My tummy hurt instantly. She said, "With that down you, it's time to stir the Christmas pudding. Come over here."

"May I take my coat upstairs first, Mrs. Joe?" I asked.

"If you must," my sister said. "But hurry."

A cold wind crept up behind me as I slipped upstairs to my attic bedroom. Its howling sound reminded me of the stranger's voice. I tried to put his threats out of my mind as I hid the bread.

I didn't waste any time getting back downstairs. Picking up the big copper spoon, I stirred the pudding. After about an hour I joined my sister and Joe in the living room.

"Warm up by the fire," she ordered, "and then get up to bed."

Huge sounds like thunder echoed through the house. "Do you hear those guns, Joe?" I asked.

He replied, "It's got to be an escaped convict."

"What's that?"

Mrs. Joe answered, "You know what it means to escape, you ninny. You do it *every day*."

I whispered to Joe, "Escaped from where?"

"A convict escaped from the prison ships a couple of days ago," Joe said. "They shot at him. Another one's trying the same."

"Who shot?" I asked.

"Drat, boy," my sister said. "Ask no questions and you'll be told no lies."

I asked, "Please, sister, who's been shooting?"

"If you must know, it's the guards on the prison ships." She frowned. My sister did not like it when I interrupted her needlework.

But I had to know. "What's a prison ship?"

The last question was too much for her. She stood up in a fury and said, "I'll tell you what, young mister. I didn't bring you up to bother people with endless questions. People are in prison because they murder and rob—all kinds of terrible behavior. Now get to bed."

"But—"

She screamed, "Bed!"

Step by step, my only thought was how I'd end up on a prison ship. The piece of bread hidden away in my room was stolen property. I'd taken it from my sister, who would punish me if she ever knew what I was about to do.

My dreams were haunted by marshes and dark prison ships. As soon as it was light outside, I crawled out of bed. With last night's dinner tucked away, I snuck into the kitchen to grab more bread and some cheese. I filled up the spare jug with my sister's Christmas punch and poured whatever was on the counter back into the bowl. I grabbed a pork pie, too, and a bone with a bit of meat still on it. With everything tied up in my pocket handkerchief, I unlocked the door to the forge. The file was easy to find among Joe's tools.

Minutes later I was outside in the foggy

morning, running for the misty marshes. I just about ran headfirst into a cow before I stumbled down into a ditch and had to climb back out.

At last I spotted the man, sleeping on a mound. I scrambled over and touched him gently on the shoulder. The man jumped up immediately. He was dressed the same, but this man wasn't the one from the graveyard!

This stranger swung a punch and fell forward. I cried out and ran fast in the direction of the old shipyard, where I found the right man waiting for me.

He grabbed my bundle, then said gruffly, "What's in the bottle, boy?"

"Something to drink."

I caught my breath as he slurped and wolfed down the food. "You swear you've brought no one with you?"

"No, sir, absolutely not!"

"Told no one where I am?"

"No!"

"It's a good thing that I believe you." He wiped his mouth on his filthy sleeve.

"Did you hear the guns last night?" I asked. "Did you see the other man?"

"Indeed, I heard the shots. Wait . . . what other man?" he said.

"I saw another convict, like you," I said.

"Where?"

"Over there." I pointed my shaking finger.

"I'll get him . . . ," my convict muttered. "Hand me that file." The man sat down and worked away at the cuff on his leg. The sight of him frightened me almost as much as the thought of my sister finding me out of the house on Christmas morning. Without even saying *good day*, I ran away. The last sound I heard was the file sawing away at the metal.

I fully expected the police to be in the kitchen waiting for me when I got home. No one was there but Mrs. Joe. She was getting everything ready for the holiday meal.

"Last night, this morning . . . Good grief, Pip! Where on earth have you been?" she demanded.

I lied, "I've been to church to hear the carols."

She said, "If I wasn't so busy being a black-smith's wife, *I'd* have time for the carols."

Joe came into the kitchen as my sister shouted, "You're not getting breakfast. I've got too much cooking to do for tonight's meal."

She stood with broom in hand and said to me, "You'd best make your way back to that church to do your duty for this family."

By the time we arrived home from church, the front door was open and waiting for company. The table was set for Christmas dinner. It looked festive and lovely. My sister had invited Mr. and Mrs. Hubble, Mr. Wopsle, and Joe's Uncle Pumblechook for dinner. As I opened the door to each of the guests, I was greeted by a cheerful, "Happy Christmas."

Mrs. Joe was in a very good mood. She talked and laughed as we all sat down to eat. I was cramped into the smallest corner of the table. Uncle Pumblechook's elbow was my closest companion. Mr. Wopsle, our church clerk, said grace. His dramatic speech lasted forever and ended with him saying, "On a day like today, there can be no other thought than being grateful for what one has."

"Indeed," echoed Pumblechook, "especially to those giving you a home." He cleared his throat. "Pip."

My sister squinted and whispered, "Do you hear that, Pip?" I kept quiet.

Mrs. Hubble said, "Why is it that the young are *never* grateful?"

Mr. Hubble replied, "It must be natural wickedness."

Joe's kindness came in the form of extra gravy for me during dinner. The more they talked about poor manners and ungrateful children, the more he poured onto my already filled plate.

"I think," Uncle said, "I should like a drink."

My sister stood up and went into the pantry. When she came back into the room, she said, "What on earth has happened to the second pork pie?"

My stomach dropped when I saw she was carrying the punch bowl I had refilled with who-knows-what. As I watched her pour Uncle a glass, my heart might actually have stopped. Pumblechook choked and spluttered on his first sip. I could stand it no longer! I stood up from the table, shouted, and ran for my life.

I got as far as the front door when I ran head-first into a group of soldiers. One held out a pair of handcuffs and said to me, "Here you are! Look sharp, come on, let's go."

CHAPTER 2

A Christmas Adventure!

Everyone came running. They were amazed to see soldiers standing there. The sergeant said, "Pardon me for interrupting your Christmas dinner. Who's Mr. Gargery? We've had an accident with the lock on these handcuffs. We need them fixed right away."

Joe stepped forward and said, "I'll need the forge for that job. It'll be two hours before it's hot enough."

"Will you start it up at once? My men will lend a hand."

Joe agreed and opened his shop. The sergeant called in the soldiers. They stood around with their arms folded behind them and waited for orders. Once I realized the cuffs weren't for me, my heart stopped racing.

"What time is it?" the sergeant asked. Uncle replied that it was half past two.

"That's not so bad," he said. "We'll still be able to catch the convicts before dusk."

"Convicts, Sergeant?" Mr. Wopsle asked.

"Yes, two. We think they're still out on the marshes and won't try to get away until it's dark. With this fog, the fools won't know we're there until they're surrounded!"

The whole group stood by the forge as Joe started hammering away. To pass the time, the sergeant told stories, and everyone—except me—seemed to enjoy themselves. At last, Joe's job was done. As the soldiers were leaving, the sergeant suggested we go with them. "Even Pip."

"As long as he doesn't get caught up in any mischief," my sister replied. Uncle Pumblechook and the Hubbles said they'd prefer to stay behind. So it was just Joe, Mr. Wopsle, and me. And the soldiers, of course.

As we walked toward the marshes, I thought about my convict. What would he think if he saw me with a group of the king's soldiers? Would he think I'd told them where he was? Would he hurt me as he'd threatened?

The fog had cleared a little, so we could see

well despite the rain. The sergeant ordered the soldiers to spread out in a long line. They walked like that until we heard shouting in the distance.

"The sound came from over there!" the sergeant shouted. "That direction, men!"

The soldiers fell out of line and ran toward the old shipyard. Joe, Mr. Wopsle, and I raced up and down the banks and through the bushes to keep up.

A soldier yelled, "The convicts! They're over there!" They rushed ahead. We could make out the sounds of a struggle as we approached the escaped men.

The sergeant pointed his gun at two men fighting at the bottom of a large ditch. He shouted, "Break it up right now!" When they didn't separate, he fired a shot into the air. "Surrender straightaway!" he yelled. To his soldiers he said, "Get in there and get them, men!"

Water splashed and mud flew in all directions

as the soldiers dove in. When they dragged the men out, I saw my convict alongside the other man I had seen that morning. I didn't want either convict to see me, so I hid behind one of the soldiers.

My convict said to the sergeant, "I was making sure you caught him. You remember that—I helped you."

The sergeant said, "It won't do you a bit of good. You're going back to the prison ship. Nothing you say or do will make one bit of difference. Now, you remember *that*."

The other convict's face was bruised and battered. "Take notice, guards," he snarled. "That man tried to hurt me."

"Ha!" said my convict. "I gave you up, and that's all. I wasn't going to let the likes of you get away."

My convict turned to the sergeant. "I escaped—I'll admit it. When I discovered he was here, I went back to catch him. Otherwise I would have been long gone by now."

"I'd have been a dead man if you soldiers hadn't shown up," the other convict said.

"Liar!" my convict shouted. "Look in his eyes and tell me he's not lying! It's written all over his face!"

"Enough!" the sergeant shouted. The convict's eyes met mine the moment I peeked out from my hiding spot. I tried to signal that none of this was my fault, but from the strange look on his face, I don't think he understood.

"That's enough out the two of you," the sergeant said to the convicts. He nodded to the soldiers and ordered, "March!"

Torches lit up the night as the soldiers moved the prisoners forward. Joe took my hand. We walked for almost an hour before coming to the docks. From there we could see the great big prison ship in the distance. One of the soldiers took the other convict on board a rowboat going back to the ship. My convict was to be next.

"I want to say something about my escape," my convict said.

"Say what you like." The sergeant looked at him coolly. "But it won't be here. You can speak once you're back on the ship."

"No, I need to clear the air. A man can't be expected to starve, can he? I'm ashamed to say I took some food from the blacksmith's."

"My goodness!" said the sergeant as he looked at Joe.

"My goodness!" said Joe as he looked at me.

"I took some pie, something to drink, some bread, and some cheese."

The sergeant said, "Blacksmith, were you missing this food?"

Joe said, "My wife noticed—at the very moment you arrived at our door! Isn't that right, Pip?"

I nodded, my eyes wide.

My convict said, "I am sorry to have taken your pie."

"That's okay," Joe said kindly. "No one deserves to starve, you poor fellow."

The prison boat, with its heavy chains and dark wood, glowed like a pirate ship. I watched my convict being taken back to it. Even though he had confessed, I didn't feel right. I knew I should tell Joe the whole truth. But my legs gave out from exhaustion before I could say a word. Joe carried me the rest of the way home.

When I woke up, I was in the parlor with our guests. They listened as Joe told the story of what happened. No one could figure out how the convict had gotten into the house to steal the food. As I drifted off to sleep, the answer was on my tongue, but the words never came out.

⌒

After the excitement of Christmas, my life settled down and continued as normal. In time I was to become a blacksmith, just like Joe. For now I was too young to be a proper apprentice. My sister hired me out to do odd jobs—scaring birds and picking up stones—and I went to school in the evenings. That's where I met Biddy. She was the granddaughter of the headmistress, and very nice. She helped me with my lessons.

One day, I was sitting in the parlor writing a letter to Joe. It was Biddy's idea—she thought it would help me learn the alphabet. The letter was messy but I passed it to him anyway.

"What a good student you are, Pip!" he said as he looked at the slate. "What printing! I can see a *J*, and an *O*, and a *Pip* in there."

"But can you read the rest?" I asked.

"The rest?"

I leaned over and read the letter out loud to him. "You don't like to read?"

"Was never taught," Joe said.

"Why not?"

"I became a blacksmith instead. Same as my father and the same as you'll become one day," Joe replied. "I took care of the family because we didn't have the money to send me to school. Then I met your sister, which meant I met you. The day I told her there was room for both of you here was the happiest day of my life."

I hugged him. His eyes twinkled and he said, "It wouldn't be so hard for you teach me what you're learning, now would it? But let's keep it a secret from your sister. It'll just make her mad." We worked together until the clock on the wall chimed eight.

"Mrs. Joe'll be home from Uncle's soon," Joe said. We stopped reading, tidied up, and stoked the fire so the room would be warm for her return. We heard the horse coming up the road, and Joe set my sister's chair in front of the fire.

She and Uncle Pumblechook came in, carrying the cold air with them.

My sister pulled off her hat. "If Pip isn't grateful for this night I don't know what to do with him!"

I tried to look as grateful as I possibly could.

She continued, "My only hope is that the whole thing doesn't spoil him. She wants this boy to go and play at her house. So he's going, and he had better behave himself."

Everybody knew who Miss Havisham was—a very rich and gloomy lady who lived in a large and scary house in town.

"I wonder how she came to know Pip?" Joe asked.

"You noodle!" my sister said to Joe. "Who said that she knows Pip? No, she knows Uncle Pumblechook. She asked if he knew a boy who could play with the girl, Estella. This could be the best thing to ever happen to Pip. Miss Havisham is rich! She might even help him later in life if he behaves. Goodness, we've got to get you ready."

I was soaped, scrubbed, and toweled within an inch of my life. The clean clothes my sister made me wear were stiff and itchy. I was to spend the night at Uncle's house before going to see Miss Havisham the next day.

"Good-bye, Joe."

"Good-bye, Pip. You take care," Joe said.

I had never spent a night apart from him since coming to live at the forge. The thought brought tears to my eyes. Out in the night with Uncle, the stars lit up the sky. They couldn't shed any light on how I ended up going to see Miss Havisham nor what I would play with once I was there.

CHAPTER 3

Pip Visits Miss Havisham

The next morning, Uncle Pumblechook walked me to Miss Havisham's. Within fifteen minutes we stopped at the biggest house I had ever seen. Made of brick, its many windows were either walled up or barred. Two large chimneys poked up from the roof, and thin black strips of smoke drifted out from each one.

We could barely see the house through the giant, overgrown courtyard. A locked gate stopped us from walking right in. Peering through it, I noticed a large, abandoned building off to the side. We rang the bell and waited. "Who's there?" a voice cried out from a window at the top of the house.

"Pumblechook and Pip," Uncle said.

A young lady came outside with the keys in her hand. She was pretty, but maybe a bit too proud. I felt embarrassed and ashamed when she looked me up and down.

"So, *this* is Pip, is it?" she said with a sneer as she unlocked the door. "I guess you might as well come in."

I left Uncle Pumblechook and followed the girl. She locked the gate behind us and we went into the courtyard. Grass grew in every nook and cranny of the pavement. She waited impatiently as I looked around. The place was falling apart.

"Manor House continues to crumble. The factory over there"—she pointed to the run-down old structure behind us—"also never gets used."

"Is that what this house is called, miss? Manor House?" I asked.

"One of its two names," she said. "The other is *Satis*, which is Greek—or Latin, or Hebrew, or all three—for 'enough.'"

"Enough House. That's a funny name."

"It's supposed to mean that whoever lives here has enough. Those were happier days. Let's go, boy, don't dawdle," she said.

Even though we looked to be the same age, I felt like my sister was there scolding me. When she called me *boy*, she spoke as if she were a queen and I were her servant. We entered the house by a side door and walked through dark hallways, lit only by the single candle she carried. For some reason, I felt nervous.

She stopped in front of a door. "Go in," she said.

"After you, miss," I said, afraid of being left alone in this scary place.

She said, "Don't be silly. I'm not going in." And she walked away.

Swallowing my fear, I knocked at the door. Someone on the other side said, "Enter."

I saw Miss Havisham for the first time. She was dressed in rich materials—silk, lace, satin— but she wore only one shoe. Drooping flowers were tucked behind her ear. Everything, even her hair, was white with a faded yellow tinge. Her clothes were meant for a much younger woman—a bride—and were too big for her bony frame.

"Who is it?" she said in a shaky voice.

"Pip. Mr. Pumblechook has brought me to play."

"Come here. Let me look at you," she ordered.

I stood in front of her, looking around so I didn't have to peer into her sunken eyes. I noticed that every clock in the room had stopped at twenty minutes to nine. I wondered why they were all broken.

"You are not afraid of a woman who hasn't seen the sun since you were born?" she asked.

"No."

"Do you know what this is?" She placed her hand on her chest.

I answered, "Your heart."

"Broken!" she shouted. "I need you to take my mind off it. Now, play." I didn't move. "Play, I said, play!"

"B-by myself?"

"Call Estella!"

I walked back and shouted "Estella!"

The snobby girl who had showed me into the house came into the room. Miss Havisham said, "Play cards with this boy to entertain me."

Estella pouted. "Play cards with a boy who has rough hands and thick boots? He's common!"

I immediately hid my hands in my pockets.

Miss Havisham picked up a handful of sparkling jewels, rich necklaces full of gems, and said to Estella, "These will be all yours one day. Is it too much for you to do as I ask? Play cards with him."

Estella picked up the deck and shuffled. I saw that Miss Havisham's other shoe lay next to her. Its perfect sole didn't have a mark on it, and the style was years out of date. The stocking on her bare foot was ragged and torn. Miss Havisham was so pale that if light was allowed into this room, she might turn to dust.

Estella won the first game. I dealt another hand. When I made a mistake, Estella told me I was foolish and silly. Miss Havisham said, "She says mean things about you, boy. What do you say about her?"

"It isn't polite, ma'am."

"Whisper in my ear."

I whispered Estella was proud, pretty, and

perhaps too mean. "I think I'd like to go home now."

"You'll never be her friend?"

"I would be her friend, but I want to go home now."

Miss Havisham said, "Finish the game first."

Estella beat me again and again. When we finished playing, Miss Havisham asked, "When shall I have you back again?"

Before I could reply, Miss Havisham told me to come back in six days. "Yes, ma'am," I said.

"Estella," she said slowly, "feed him. Let him roam around the courtyard before he leaves."

I followed Estella and her candle through the house. The sunlight almost blinded me when she opened the door. "Wait here, boy."

The door slammed, and I stood alone in the courtyard. When she returned, Estella set down bread and meat on a stone as if I were a dog. Feelings of anger and hurt welled up inside me, and I started to cry. Estella made fun of me, which made me cry more. I ran away to the factory and kicked the wall a few times before I left to go home.

When I got home, my sister started asking questions. I felt awful because of the way Estella had treated me, but I did my best to answer. Uncle Pumblechook arrived, and he asked how it went. I said fine.

"That's no answer—what happened exactly?"

My sister glared at me. Uncle Pumblechook said, "Don't lose your temper, Mrs. Joe. I'll handle this. What did you think of Miss Havisham?"

I sputtered, "She's t-tall."

"There, that wasn't so hard, was it, Pip? What was she doing when you went inside?"

"Sitting on a black velvet chair."

Both my sister and Uncle Pumblechook cooed at the thought of a black velvet chair.

"Miss Estella," I said, "handed her cake on

gold plates and water in gold cups. Everything looked delicious."

Uncle Pumblechook asked, "Who else was there?

"Four dogs," I answered.

"Large or small?"

"Huge," I said. "They ate out of silver dishes."

"Dogs eating from silver dishes!" my sister and Uncle Pumblechook exclaimed.

I would have continued my story if Joe had not come in for his dinner. My sister and Uncle Pumblechook talked about my good fortune all through the meal. They were thrilled Miss Havisham might take me under her wing.

After dinner, I went into the forge to find Joe and told him the truth.

"Why did you lie?" he asked gently.

The words came pouring out. I told him about Miss Havisham and how Estella called me common. I told him I didn't want to disappoint my sister, and about my rough hands and thick boots.

Joe paused. "Lying won't make you any less common, Pip." He continued, "Don't tell any more lies. You can't go straight if you're crooked. If you live well and honest, everything will be fine."

I left him then and went up to my room. I wondered, if I was common, how common was Joe? Before today, I had never considered myself common. I had never imagined how different people's lives were from my own.

I did not know what it meant to be a young gentleman, but I wanted badly for Estella to see me in that way. Before crawling into bed, I promised myself she'd never see me cry again, no matter how much she hurt my feelings.

CHAPTER 4

A Stranger Comes to the Three Jolly Bargemen

After school the next evening, my sister sent me to fetch Joe at the Three Jolly Bargemen. The restaurant was just down the road from our house. I found Joe inside by the fire with a stranger and Mr. Wopsle.

The stranger said, "So, you're the blacksmith?" He rubbed his leg in a very strange manner when he spoke.

"Yes," Joe answered. "And this is Mr. Wopsle, our church clerk, right, Pip?"

"Yes, Joe," I answered, looking at the man's

strange hat. Underneath it he wore a hand-kerchief that covered his hair.

The stranger said, "Pip? That's his given name?"

Joe said, "He gave it to himself as a baby and it stuck."

"Your son?"

Joe smiled. "He's my nephew."

"Drinks for my friends, please," the stranger said as he stared at me. When the drinks arrived, the stranger pulled something odd out of his pocket to stir his drink. It was the file I'd stolen last Christmas! Was this stranger my convict? How could that be? Spellbound, I couldn't take my eyes away. After he was sure I had noticed the file, he returned it to his pocket. Then the stranger changed the conversation to turnips.

Later, when Joe stood up to go, he said, "Stop a moment, Mr. Gargery. I've got something in my pocket for the boy." He pulled out some coins, wrapped them in paper, and handed them to me. "Remember, these are just for you," he told me.

Wednesday came and I was back at Miss Havisham's. Estella opened the door and said coldly, "You're to come this way."

We wound along a series of passageways, chased by shadows from her single candle. Finally, we came to a door that opened up into the back courtyard. Three ladies and two gentlemen stood by the clock on the outside wall—also stopped at twenty minutes to nine. Everyone turned to look at us.

Estella pointed to an ugly corner. "You stand over there while I go talk to Sarah Pocket and her brother Matthew." She left.

When a bell rang in the distance some time later, Estella said, "Let's go, boy."

Sarah and Matthew Pocket and the rest of the party watched as we left. The others were merrily clinking their teacups and enjoying tiny pieces of cake. When we rounded the corner, I could no longer hear them.

Suddenly, Estella stopped and asked, "Are you still upset from last week?"

"No," I replied.

"I'll *make* you cry again."

We were silent the rest of the way to Miss Havisham's room. "In you go, boy," Estella said. She walked away, her candle bobbing up and down the dark hallway.

"It's that time again, is it, Pip?" the old woman asked. She stopped me before I said anything. "What will you play today?"

"Anything you'd like, Miss Havisham."

"Fine," she said. "Let's go into the other room across the hall."

I crossed the staircase and went into a dark room lit only by a fire. Smoke hung in the air like the fog on the marshes. A big room, it must have been grand once. Now the furniture was dusty and falling apart. Great cobwebs hung from a large table, and mice rattled around in the walls.

A great bride's cake was displayed on the table. Cobwebs draped over that, too. "Walk me around the ballroom," Miss Havisham demanded.

After a few laps, she said, "Call Estella."

I did, and Estella came in with the company from the courtyard. Each asked Miss Havisham how she was and told her how well she looked, all while we toured around the room. Miss Havisham never said a word. We didn't even stop walking once they were gone. Their good-byes were left unanswered.

"Today is my birthday," Miss Havisham said.

I was about to give my good wishes when she continued, "I don't like to talk about it. I know why *they* were here. They come every year."

When Estella came back from showing the group out, Miss Havisham said, "I'd like to watch the two of you play cards."

Estella didn't talk to me through a single one of our six games.

"See you in a week, Pip," Miss Havisham said. "Show him out, Estella."

Outside, Estella set down food as she had done before, leaving me alone to wander in the garden.

"Who let you in?" said a pale young gentleman.

I replied, "Miss Estella."

He shouted, "You can't just wander around. Follow me."

The boy was so strange that I did as he said. We walked a few paces before he turned around, raised his fists, and said, "Put 'em up!"

Hopping on one foot, then the next, he poked me, pulled my hair, and then raced off. "Now we have a reason to fight."

We ended up boxing in a far corner of the garden. Every time I knocked the young man down, he got back up. Once in a while he'd pour water over himself with a sponge from a bucket nearby. After many punches, he finally threw the sponge up in the air. "You've won!" he declared.

"May I help you up?" I said.

"No, thanks," he said.

"Um, good afternoon, then?" I said.

"Same to you."

I made my way back to the other courtyard where Estella was waiting. "Good-bye," she said impatiently as she opened the gate.

I walked out slowly thinking to myself, *What a strange day. An unhappy birthday party, a fight, and Estella still doesn't like me.*

I was sure the next time I went to Miss Havisham's I would get in trouble for fighting. Village boys like me just couldn't go around punching young gentleman. What if Miss Havisham didn't let me come back? How common would Estella think I was if she knew I beat up that young man?

A week later, as I stood in front of Miss Havisham's house, I wondered if I would see the strange boy. The afternoon passed by as it always did. Estella and I played cards. Miss Havisham had me walk her about the ballroom. No one mentioned that a boy other than me had ever been there.

∾

Over the next few months I spent much of my time at Miss Havisham's. Most afternoons we walked. Sometimes, if she was tired, I pushed her around in an old garden chair with wheels. She asked me a lot of questions, and I always answered her honestly. But Estella treated me as poorly as ever. Even so, I longed for us to be friends. So I tried to act differently, more like a young gentleman should, in an effort to win her affection.

One day Miss Havisham said, "What's the name of your blacksmith?"

"Joe Gargery, ma'am,"

"Bring him with you next time. I'd like to meet him."

Two days later the pair of us arrived at the gate. Joe was as nervous and uncomfortable as ever in his good clothes. Estella silently opened the gate and led us upstairs. Joe held tight to his hat, as if it weighed far more than it did. I wondered why Miss Havisham had called for Joe.

"This is your uncle, Pip?" Miss Havisham said.

"Pip, I am married to your sister," Joe said to me.

"Joe," I said, "you can just talk to Miss Havisham."

"Pip," he said, "you was always meant to come work for me."

I was embarrassed. Joe kept muddling his words and shuffling his feet. He kept directing his answers to me instead of Miss Havisham.

Joe said, "You'll become a blacksmith and all will be right in this world."

Miss Havisham said, "Pip's a very good boy, and I've got something for him, Mr. Gargery." She held out a bag full of silver coins. "Good-bye, Pip. You be good for Joe."

I asked, "Am I not to come back?"

"No," she said, "you'll start working with Joe now."

I took the bag she held out, as Joe refused to move. "Estella will show you both out."

How Joe managed to move his feet out of the room, I'll never know.

My sister was waiting for us at Uncle Pumblechook's store. When we got there, Joe said, "That Miss Havisham was very happy with Pip. She's given us a present."

"What do you mean?" my sister asked.

"It's twenty-five pounds!" Joe said.

"Uncle!" my sister shouted. "All of this is thanks to you!" Pumblechook smiled and said it was his pleasure.

We walked to the courthouse that afternoon and signed the papers that made me an apprentice to Joe. It was official: I was on my way to becoming a blacksmith. My life would have more rules than ever now. It was serious business to be an apprentice. It meant that I would have to learn a real trade.

My sister and Uncle Pumblechook said we needed to celebrate, so we went to the Three Jolly Bargemen for dinner. They were pleased, but I knew I'd never enjoy being a blacksmith. I had liked the idea of it once, before I knew Miss Havisham and Estella. Before I felt ashamed of who I was and where I came from. Before I knew a boy could grow up to be a young gentleman.

CHAPTER 5

An Accident at Home

Now that I worked in the forge, I no longer went to school or to see Miss Havisham. Biddy helped me keep up with my lessons so I could teach Joe, but I missed my visits to Manor House. One day Joe and I were bent over my slate and I said, "Do you think I should visit Miss Havisham? I'd like to thank her properly."

Joe said, "She might think you want something. You were paid handsomely, Pip."

"Still, it's my birthday tomorrow. May I have a half holiday?"

"If you think it's best, then you should go."

The next day when Orlick, Joe's assistant, heard that Joe had given me a half holiday, he wanted one, too. "I suppose, to be fair, you can both go," Joe said.

My sister was standing in the garden and heard the whole conversation. "You don't deserve a half holiday, Orlick, you lazy man!"

"You're not my master," Orlick sneered, "you mean, sour-faced old lady."

"The names he's calling me!" my sister shouted.

"Your wife is a nasty woman," Orlick yelled to Joe.

"Quiet!" Joe said. "Pip, off you go before even more trouble starts."

Manor House hadn't changed in the months I'd been away. But I was surprised when Sarah Pocket answered the gate instead of Estella.

"What are you doing here?" she asked.

"I could ask you the same question," I replied. "Where's Estella?"

"She's gone to school, if you must know. What's your business here?"

"I've come to wish Miss Havisham well."

Sarah said, "She won't give you anything, you know."

Sarah called upstairs to see if she could let me in. Minutes later, I stood in front of Miss Havisham, who said, "I hope you haven't come here thinking you're getting more presents, even though it's your birthday," she said.

I must have looked surprised because she said, "Foolish boy, I know what *day* it is."

I said, "I don't expect anything. I just wanted to thank you properly for what you've done."

No sooner had I said those words than I was back on the street. On the lonely walk home, I admired a shop window in town. I thought about all of the things I would buy if I were a rich gentleman. Mr. Wopsle happened to walk by, too. Then we ran into Orlick.

"The guns are going again," Orlick said. "More prisoners have escaped."

As we passed the Three Jolly Bargemen, Uncle Pumblechook came running outside. "There's been some trouble at your house, Pip. Let's get over there now!"

When the four of us arrived, we found the entire village in our kitchen with Joe. The group stepped back to reveal my sister terribly hurt and not moving on the floor.

Joe had called for help the moment he found her. The house was undisturbed. The only clue was the prison cuff lying next to her on the floor. We all wondered who had hurt my sister. Joe guessed the iron cuff belonged to one of the escaped convicts. Had the two prisoners we saw on the marshes so long ago escaped again?

The doctor put my poor sister to bed. She had

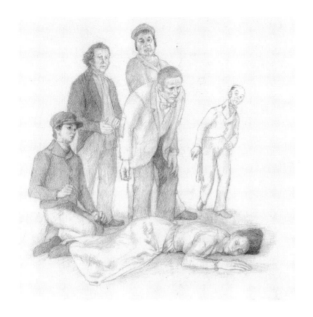

suffered a very serious hit on the head. Weeks went by before she was even able to sit up, never mind see or speak properly. Joe was so upset. Mr. Wopsle suggested Biddy could come and live with us to help around the house. Joe and I both thought this was a good idea. Biddy was kind and helped my sister a great deal.

cx

My life fell into a routine over the next three years: I worked with Joe in the shop and visited Miss Havisham on my birthday. On Sunday afternoons Joe stayed in with my sister while Biddy and I walked through the marshes.

"Biddy," I said, "I need to make a confession. More than anything I wish that I was a young gentleman."

She said, "Not a blacksmith?"

"That was never my choice."

"Why? What's made you so unhappy?"

I confessed that I wanted to impress Estella. Biddy said that was silly. She reminded me it was ungrateful to wish for a different life when people like Joe were so kind to me. I didn't say anything, but I couldn't help wanting what I didn't have.

A few days later, Joe and I were in the Three Jolly Bargemen. A man shouted, "I hear there's a blacksmith among you. Is Joe Gargery here?"

"I'm here," Joe said.

"Do you have an apprentice, known as Pip?"

"That's me," I said.

"Nice to meet you," the man said. "Perhaps we could go to your house to discuss a matter in private?"

We left the Three Jolly Bargemen and were soon sitting in our parlor, looking at one another in confusion.

"My name is Mr. Jaggers," the man began. "I'm a lawyer acting on behalf of someone who wishes their identity to remain a secret."

The room was dark, so Mr. Jaggers shifted to see us better. "I know Pip's your apprentice," he said to Joe. "Being a blacksmith would be a good and honest life for him. But the person I work for thinks the boy has great expectations."

"Indeed!" Joe said, surprised.

"This person has asked me to tell Pip that he will inherit a great deal of money one day." Mr. Jaggers turned to me. "You now have a benefactor, Pip—do you understand? Someone who plans to give you a fortune."

He continued, "But before Pip comes into this money, my client wants him to be brought up like a gentleman."

I was too excited to say a word. Mr. Jaggers said, "You'll be moving to London to begin a new life."

My heart started to beat very fast. My benefactor had to be Miss Havisham!

"I have instructions that you are always to keep the name Pip." He laughed. "That's not so hard, is it?" I shook my head.

"The name of your benefactor will remain a secret. It may not be revealed to you until years from now. You must not try to find out who this person is. You also shouldn't ask any questions. Understood?"

"Yes," I said.

"Your education will be paid for. You will

be placed with Mr. Matthew Pocket." I nodded.

Mr. Jaggers noticed I recognized the name. "You know this man?"

"I have met his sister, sir. She works at the largest house in town. I once had reasons to visit there."

"Right." He quickly changed the subject. "You'll need new clothes, books, and other supplies."

He handed me an envelope. "You look shocked, Mr. Gargery."

"I am!" Joe said. "I will miss the boy terribly. But if it's what's best for Pip . . ."

"In one week's time, Pip, you'll take a coach and come to my offices in London. Here's the address." Mr. Jaggers stood up and handed me a card. "I shall see you then."

He was almost out the door before I asked, "I know I'm not to speak of it, but would it be okay if I went to town to say good-bye to a certain person? Someone who lives in that very big house?"

"That's fine, Pip," Mr. Jaggers said as Joe showed him the way out. By the time I left the parlor, Joe was in the living room with my sister and Biddy.

"Have you told them, Joe?" I asked.

"I thought you'd want to," he said.

"I think you should," I said.

"Pip's going to become a gentleman and come into a great fortune. He'll never have to work a day in his life."

Biddy dropped her sewing. No one spoke for a long time until everyone stood up to congratulate me.

"I cannot say anything about the person who's helping me. I don't know who it is and we mustn't guess. It's a secret."

Biddy and Joe promised they would keep the secret, and my sister nodded, too. What a surprising day! On the one hand, I was excited to become a gentleman. On the other, everything was about to change—whether or not I was ready.

As I walked through the marshes the next day, I couldn't help but think of my convict. With my back to the stone wall of the churchyard, I fell asleep. When I woke up, I saw a very sad Joe in front of me.

"Time for dinner, Pip," he said.

We set out for home. I said, "Joe, I'll never forget you. But I've always wanted to be a gentleman."

"Have you, now?" Joe asked.

"It's a shame we won't be able to carry on with our lessons."

"I suppose I was never meant for schooling and you were never meant to be a blacksmith," Joe said kindly.

After dinner I tried to talk to Biddy about

Joe, and what I wanted for him—to have better manners and to learn more.

"That's unkind to say, Pip. Joe's the dearest man. His manners are just fine," she said angrily.

We argued. I told her she was jealous of my good fortune. She said I was mean and selfish. We parted angrily and never had a good chance to talk about it again. I was so busy preparing to go to London.

Everywhere I went people congratulated me on my good fortune. They treated me differently. So I started to act more like a gentleman. The days flew by. But I knew I had to make time to see Miss Havisham.

When Sarah Pocket came to the gate, I said, "It's not a day I usually visit, but I'm moving to London and I want to say good-bye."

Sarah went upstairs to make sure it was okay, and then took me in to see Miss Havisham.

"Pip!" she said. "I have heard your good news. You leave tomorrow?"

"Yes, Miss Havisham."

"You've been adopted in secret by a rich person, have you?"

"Yes, Miss Havisham."

"Be good," she said, "and deserve this kindness."

Those last few nights I spent at home were some of my happiest. Biddy, Joe, and I laughed and talked late into the nights. Biddy and I pretended we'd never had our fight. Neither of us wanted to ruin my final few days at the forge. On my last evening, we had a special dinner. Just like at Christmas, Joe spoiled me with too much gravy.

My heart was heavy as I climbed the stairs to my small attic bedroom. Joe and Biddy wanted to walk me to the coach in the morning, but I had told them no. I had to go alone.

Sad and scared, my dreams were filled with coaches going to the wrong place, with me getting lost in the big city. When I woke just before dawn, I got dressed and looked out my window one last time.

Biddy was up early with my breakfast. I could hear her downstairs. Yet I couldn't leave my room. I buckled and unbuckled my suitcase. I packed and repacked my new shirts.

"Pip," Biddy called, "come down for breakfast. You'll miss your coach!"

I ate as quickly as possible, not tasting a bit of my food. "Well," I said when I was finished, "I supposed I must be off!"

I kissed my sister, quickly threw my arms around Joe's neck, and gave Biddy a peck on the cheek. I grabbed my suitcase and left. I was barely on the street when I heard the door open. When I turned around, Biddy and Joe were throwing old shoes at me for good luck.

I stopped and waved my hat. Dear Joe waved his strong arm above his head and called, "Hurray! Pip, hurray!" Before I turned back, Biddy covered her face with her apron because she was crying.

As I strolled past the Three Jolly Bargemen, I thought, *That wasn't as hard as I thought it was going to be.*

The town was quiet, and the mist was lifting, as if it were showing me everything I'd be missing. Biddy, Joe, my sister—they were all I'd ever known. I burst into tears from the shock of actually leaving home. What was London going to be like? There was so much I didn't know.

As I wept, I thought, *I should have let Joe walk me to the coach. I could have said a proper good-bye.*

The coachman took my suitcase, and I paused with one foot on the step. *Should I turn around right now and go home?*

"In you get, young sir," the coachman said. "We've got a schedule to keep."

It was too late to change my mind. My thoughts raced over everything I'd left behind. As I looked out the window, I saw a brand-new world.

This is the end of the first stage of
Pip's Great Expectations.

CHAPTER 6

A New Life in London

༄

Five hours later, I was in a coach taking me to Mr. Jaggers's office. The gloomy street frightened me a little, so I quickly went inside and introduced myself to the clerk.

"Mr. Jaggers is in court, young sir, but you're to wait here for him."

There were many people crowded into the room waiting to see him. When Mr. Jaggers finally arrived, he talked with everyone else first before he approached me. After leading me back into his private room, he washed his hands and face and said, "At last, Pip, you've arrived. You're to go to Barnard's Inn to see Mr. Pocket's son, Herbert. Stay there until Monday, when you'll go to the Pockets's house in Hammersmith. You won't be at school full-time, so we'll have to sort out a place for you to stay here in London, too."

He continued, "Here's your allowance. My clerk, Wemmick, will be keeping tabs on you in case you run into any trouble."

"Should I call for a cab?" I asked.

"Wemmick can walk you over. It's not far."

Mr. Wemmick smiled as we stepped out onto the street. He asked if I'd ever been to London before. When I said no, he chuckled. "I was new here once."

A short man with a square face, Wemmick had a nose that looked like it was carved out of wood. "Funny to think about that now when I know the city so well," he said.

The gate for Barnard's Inn opened into a

dismal square complete with dismal trees and dismal birds. Dirty windows with FOR RENT signs, broken flowerpots, and a layer of dust completed the scene. I could see no earthly reason why *anyone* might want to live here.

Mr. Wemmick led me up a rickety set of stairs. I thought they would collapse beneath our feet. We came to a door with a note that said, *Be right back!*

"I suppose Herbert didn't think you'd be early," Mr. Wemmick said. "Do you need me to wait here in the hallway with you?"

"No, I'll be fine."

"I'm sure we'll meet again." Mr. Wemmick started back downstairs. "Good day!"

As I waited, I wrote my name on a dirty window and thought, *London is not what I expected.* Five, then ten, then thirty minutes passed. Finally, I heard the sound of shoes on the stairs. A young man in a suit identical to mine soon stood before me. He looked very familiar to me. "Pip?" he said.

"Herbert?"

"Dear me!" he said. "I thought you would take the afternoon coach. I've been out getting us some fruit."

Herbert pushed, pulled, and attacked the door as if it were a wild beast. At last it opened.

"Come in, come in!" he shouted excitedly. "It's a small place." He showed me around. "Tomorrow, I thought—well, Mr. Jaggers thought—we could take a walk around London . . ."

Herbert's voice trailed off as he looked at me more closely. "Why, it's you! From that day in Miss Havisham's garden."

Suddenly I recognized him. "And you're the pale young gentleman!"

We laughed. "Of all places, Pip! How have you come to be here?"

I replied, "I'm to come into a fortune one day. My benefactor wants me to become a gentleman."

Herbert was cheerful and chatty and made me feel right at home. After dinner we ate strawberries and swapped stories about Miss Havisham. I even told Herbert that I thought she was the one helping me.

"It's a secret," I said.

"It's safe with me," he said. "Do you know the story of Miss Havisham's life?"

"I know she was supposed to be married."

Herbert told me her father had owned a factory, the one on the grounds of Manor House. "She was popular, always attending balls and parties," he continued. "She met a young man who wasn't very nice. On the day they were to be married he didn't show up. Stole her money and sent a letter instead."

I gasped. "He just left her?"

Herbert nodded. "At that very minute all the clocks in Manor House were stopped."

"What happened to him?"

"He fell onto hard times," Herbert said. "Might have ended up in jail. Soon after, Miss Havisham adopted Estella."

Before I could ask about Estella, Herbert started telling me about his plans to own a shipping empire. We spent the rest of the night dreaming of the future.

Monday came, and we went by coach to Hammersmith to meet Mr. Pocket, Herbert's dad. He was to be my teacher. As we walked into the garden, we saw Herbert's six brothers and sisters tumbling around.

"Mother," Herbert called, "this is young Mr. Pip."

At that moment, Mr. Pocket came rushing out of the house, shouting, "Good to see you, Pip! Hope you're glad to see us, too!" He was a young-looking man despite his gray hair, and was as easygoing and friendly as Herbert.

He showed me upstairs to my airy, pleasant room. It even had a little sitting area next to the desk. We left my suitcase behind and knocked on two similar doors. My fellow students, Startop and Drummle, came out to say hello. Bentley Drummle was heavyset and unpleasant. He was the opposite of Startop, who was thin and looked like the type of boy who was always reading.

Mr. Pocket said, "I'll leave you boys to chat."

Drummle said, "Should we take the boats out for a row?"

Startop said, "As long as I can sit and read."

"As if you ever do anything else," Drummle said, sulking. "Pip, you'll row, right?"

"I suppose, yes."

We found Herbert, and the four of us had a bit of fun on the river, despite Drummle's sour mood. We had just stowed the boats when it was time for dinner. A lively occasion, there was fuss over a missing cook and misbehaving children. Afterward, Mr. Pocket sighed and said, "Pip, I do hope you'll like it here."

"I already know that I will," I said.

Over the next few days, Mr. Pocket and I went back and forth between London and Hammersmith to buy new school supplies. I'd be taking general lessons and wouldn't be training for any specific career. Not like when I was Joe's apprentice. Mr. Pocket was a very good teacher, and I loved learning from him.

I spent half my time in Hammersmith, and the other half in London, with Herbert. The arrangement suited me just fine. Herbert was becoming one of my closest friends. I had finally found happiness in London.

One afternoon, I realized it had been some time since I'd seen Wemmick. I decided to go to the office to see if he wanted to have dinner.

"I'll be done here in a few minutes," Wemmick said. "Then why don't we go to my house?"

Along the way, Wemmick said, "I think Mr. Jaggers plans to invite you and your friends to dinner tomorrow night."

"All of us?"

"There's four of you, right? Herbert, Startop, Drummle, and you." Even though I didn't think of Drummle as a pal, I said yes.

"Look, I've got to warn you. Mr. Jaggers's housekeeper, Molly, is very strange."

"Strange how?"

"She's good at her job, mind you. But she has a dark past. She was in a great deal of trouble with the law. Mr. Jaggers fixed the situation."

Wemmick lived in Walworth. We took a series of back lanes until we arrived at the smallest house I had ever seen. "I built my 'castle' myself," Wemmick said. "On Sundays I even run a flag up the flagpole."

"It's lovely," I said.

He pulled down the large plank he used as a drawbridge. We crossed a moat, and then a garden many times the size of the house. "I created all of this!" he claimed, cheerily. "I am my own jack-of-all-trades."

Once inside, Wemmick introduced me to his "aged parent." That's what he lovingly called his father. The elderly man was hard of hearing, so I tipped my hat to him. He chuckled.

We had a delicious fish dinner and great conversation. "Might as well spend the night, Pip," Wemmick said when the clock struck midnight. "It's a long walk back to Barnard's Inn."

I said good night to the aged parent and followed Wemmick to a room upstairs. As I closed the door, I thought about how I had never laughed so much in my life as I had during dinner. Wemmick was serious and harsh while at work in Mr. Jaggers's office. But at home he was an inventor, a carpenter, a plumber, a gardener, and a bit of a clown. I felt special knowing both sides of him.

The next morning I went into the office with Wemmick. "Pip," Mr. Jaggers called. "Good to see you. How about coming to my house for dinner tonight with your three pals? You may come here first, and then we'll go to my house."

Drummle, Startop, Herbert, and I arrived at six o'clock sharp. Mr. Jaggers led us through the crowded streets. At last we came upon a house in good need of a cleaning and a paint job.

"Follow me, boys. In you come, don't be shy," he said. We walked upstairs to the third floor where Mr. Jaggers's housekeeper had already set out our meal. As the boys helped themselves to a drink, Mr. Jaggers pulled me aside. "Pip, I'm afraid I don't know who's who—except Herbert, of course. Who's the spidery-looking fellow?"

"Who?" I said.

"The blotchy, sprawly, sulky one."

"Oh, Drummle. The one with the softer face is Startop."

"Right. I like the look of him," he said. I didn't pretend to understand why, and was glad when the housekeeper motioned for us all to sit. I stole a glance at her and noticed that Molly was tall and very pale, with large eyes and long hair. I couldn't put my finger on it, but there was something familiar about her. Once she served our food, Mr. Jaggers motioned for her to leave.

Dinner went off without a hitch. Mr. Jaggers mainly listened as we boys chatted freely. Of course Drummle bragged about his rowing, and we all rolled our eyes. This upset him enough to remark that we spent too much money, and should be ashamed of ourselves.

I said, "Should you be pointing fingers? You

don't have any of your allowance left, either! Didn't you borrow money from Startop last week?"

"I'll pay him back!" Drummle shouted.

"I never said you wouldn't!" I yelled. "You wouldn't loan us the shirt off your back if we needed it."

"Quite right," he continued. "I wouldn't loan anything to anyone!"

Startop said something funny to stop us from arguing. Mr. Jaggers announced, "All right, boys, it's half past nine. Time to call it a night."

Before we left, I apologized to Mr. Jaggers for our rough behavior.

"No worries, Pip. See you soon." We all spilled out of Mr. Jaggers's home into the misty London air. I decided that from then on I would keep my distance from Drummle. I linked arms with Herbert and we walked back to Barnard's Inn.

CHAPTER 7

A Letter from Home

∾

Dear Pip,

Joe asked me to write this letter. He's coming into London. He'll call for you at Barnard's Inn on Tuesday morning at 9 o'clock. Your poor sister is the same as before. We talk about you every night. Hope you're doing well.

Yours truly,
Biddy

The letter came on Monday, which meant Joe would be arriving tomorrow. I had mixed feelings about Joe's visit. My life was so different now, I didn't know if he would fit into it. I wanted to send a note telling him not to come.

Tuesday came, and it rained. As I heard Joe's boots clomping up the stairs, I wanted to hide. Instead I answered the knock at the door. Joe shouted, "Hello, Pip! You've grown!"

His good, honest face glowed as he heartily shook my hand. "Good to see you, Joe," I said. "Please, give me your hat."

"Oh, it's fine where it fell." The hat sat on the floor between us. I told Joe he looked well. He said, "Your sister's the same. Biddy, too. But Wopsle has left the church to become an actor!"

"An actor?'" I said.

Joe handed me a crumpled program.

"Did you see the play?" I asked.

"Indeed, I did," he answered. As Joe described the play, I tried to pull both him and his hat

inside. Herbert called out when he saw Joe in the hallway, "So nice to meet you! Won't you join us at the table?"

Herbert asked, "Coffee or tea, Mr. Gargery?" Joe set his hat on the mantel.

"Whichever you'd like," Joe answered quietly.

"Coffee, then," Herbert said.

Joe said, "Fine choice. But don't you find coffee hurts your stomach?"

"We'll have tea instead." Herbert poured and we sat down to breakfast.

Joe's hat fell off the mantel. He stood up, put it in the very same spot, and it tumbled down again.

Herbert asked, "When did you come into town, Mr. Gargery?"

"Were it yesterday afternoon?" Joe coughed into his hand as if the London air had already made him ill. "Yes, yes it were——"

His hat fell from the mantel for the third time and he had to rescue it once more. Joe's behavior was beginning to embarrass me. I was relieved when Herbert set off for the day.

Joe turned to me. "Now that it's just the two of us, sir, I've got something to——"

"Joe," I snapped, "there's no need to call me *sir*. What is it? Why have you come?"

Joe told a long, rambling story about the Three Jolly Bargemen before getting to the point.

"You see, Pip, she wants to see you."

"Who?"

"Miss Havisham."

"Why didn't you tell me that right away? You know how important Miss Havisham is to me!" I said sharply.

"Now, wait a minute, let me remember . . . Something about the girl being pleased if she could see you?"

"Estella?"

"Seems she's back from school and would be glad for your company. It was Biddy's idea for me to tell you in person."

Breakfast was finished, and he thanked me for the meal. As he stood up to leave, he said "Some people are just blacksmiths, I suppose. I'm not fit for these clothes or this city. Doubt that I'll be back, but I hope you'll come see us at the forge."

He touched my forehead and left. As soon

as I realized that dear Joe would never come to see me again, I rushed out into the street to find him. He was already gone. I felt awful about the way I had treated him.

I booked a coach to take me home the very next day so I could see Miss Havisham and Estella. I was ashamed of how poorly I had treated Joe. But still, I didn't want to go home. So I booked a room at the Blue Boar hotel and walked the long way around so I wouldn't have to pass the forge.

Walking the cold, foggy streets, I thought, *Miss Havisham has given me a wonderful new life in London. How will I ever repay her?*

I decided right then and there that I'd be the one to rebuild Manor House. I'd tear down the cobwebs and be her hero. When I arrived at the gate, it gave me quite a shock to find Orlick standing there.

"What are you doing?" I said.

Orlick stared at me. "There are more changes in life than just yours, Pip," he replied.

"How long has it been since you've left the forge?" I asked.

"How long since *you've* left the forge? It's my job now to open the gate. You might as well come through," he said.

Even after all this time, I knew Manor House couldn't have changed. But the dark staircase no longer made me frightened. I had been up and down it so many times. I knocked on Miss Havisham's door. She called, "Why, that's Pip's knock! Please come in!"

She was in her chair next to the old table, wearing the same old dress. The white shoe that had never been worn sat atop the table beside her. When I greeted her in my new gentlemanly manner, she smiled, "You kiss my hand as if I were a queen. Well?"

I said, "You wanted to see me?"

Miss Havisham tilted her head, and I noticed there a young lady in the room. *"Well?"* Miss Havisham said.

It was Estella! She, too, gave me her hand to kiss. I said, "It's very nice to see you."

"Hasn't she changed, Pip?" Miss Havisham said.

"I didn't even recognize her," I replied.

"Isn't Pip less common?" she asked Estella.

Estella laughed and said, "Yes, the boy's not as rough around the edges."

She proudly told me about coming home from France. "I'm to go to London soon," she said in that bored way she spoke. Even so, I still wanted to impress her—that never changed.

Miss Havisham announced that I was to stay at Manor House for the day. Then she sent the two of us outside. We walked through the weeds and grass.

"Do you remember the fight you had out

here with Herbert?" she asked.

"He and I are great friends now," I said.

"You had no idea then you would become a gentleman, did you?"

"None," I said softly. "My life's very different now." Walking was difficult because the garden was so overgrown.

"Do you remember how you would leave food for me on the steps and walk away without saying anything?" I asked.

She laughed, "Oh, Pip, don't be silly. I would never do such a thing."

How did she not remember this detail of my every visit? I recalled everything that happened between us. Right then I knew Estella would never be as fond of me as I was of her.

"Are you going to start crying?" she teased. "Let's go inside. I'm tired."

Estella went upstairs to change for dinner. Miss Havisham pulled me aside and said, "You must *always* be her friend, Pip. Even if she treats you horribly or is very mean. Promise me you'll still be her friend."

"I promise, Miss Havisham," I said.

Miss Havisham was so excited, she rose up out of her chair and almost fell over. I caught her and helped her sit back down. When I turned I was surprised to see Mr. Jaggers standing there.

"What are you doing here, Pip?" he asked.

"I arrived this morning to see Miss Havisham and Estella."

"She's a fine young lady, isn't she?" Mr. Jaggers said of Estella.

For some reason this annoyed Miss Havisham. "Oh, shut up, both of you, and get down to dinner."

Estella and Sarah Pocket joined us, but Miss Havisham stayed upstairs. After the meal, the four of us played cards. Miss Havisham came down to watch, just as she had when I was a boy.

Before I left, Miss Havisham pulled me aside. "Pip, you must visit with Estella in London." Of course, I agreed. I said good night to everyone and went back to the Blue Boar for the night.

Back in London the next day, I told Herbert about the strange evening and my promise to Miss Havisham.

"It's doesn't sound that odd, Pip," he said. "Seems to me she's just looking out for Estella."

"I hope my inheritance isn't dependent on Estella's friendship. She's never liked me."

"Mr. Jaggers has never said so, right?" Herbert asked.

"No, absolutely not," I answered.

"Then you've got nothing to worry about. Forget about silly, snobby Estella. Everything will turn out all right. I know it."

CHAPTER 8

Another Two Letters

❧

One afternoon as I was reading at home, a short letter with no greeting came for me:

I am to come to London tomorrow on the midday coach. Meet me. Miss Havisham sends her regards.

—Estella

The morning of Estella's visit found me pacing the station far too early. I was a bundle of nerves. My palms were sweating and my stomach was full of butterflies. I wondered, *What will we talk about? Will I be good company?*

Instead of waiting in the station, I decided to walk over and visit Wemmick. Together we ran some errands for Mr. Jaggers. I returned to the station to find Estella waving at me from the coach window.

She pointed out her luggage, and I arranged for it to be collected. "Where are you off to?" I asked.

"To Richmond," she said. "Miss Havisham told me to get a carriage because ten miles is too far to walk. You'll accompany me, of course, and arrange everything." She handed me a small, pretty pouch that contained her money.

"I'll send for the carriage. Will you rest here for a minute?" I asked.

"Yes. I would like some tea and for you to spend a little while with me. I want to see a bit of London."

When we were seated in the tearoom, I asked, "Why are you going to Richmond?"

"I am to live with an important society woman. She'll introduce me to the right people."

"It'll be nice to meet so many different people."

"Perhaps," she answered. She paused for a moment, and we were silent. "Do you like it at the Pockets's?"

"I do," I replied. "My studies are going well. I have discovered that I love to read."

Estella cackled in that mean way of hers. "You know," she said, "somebody there is making fun of you behind your back. He sends anonymous letters to Miss Havisham to tell her all of your mistakes."

"It doesn't bother me," I said. "I'm sure Miss Havisham knows the truth about me. In fact, I think I know who might have sent them—my classmate Drummle. He's always looking for trouble."

Estella smirked. "Yes, I'm sure Miss Havisham realizes there's nothing to worry about. We'd better get to that carriage."

We toured around London, and I showed Estella the sights. Hours later, after I dropped her off in Richmond, sadness washed over me. The day had been fun, and I already missed her. Our time together was too short.

உ

A couple of days later, Herbert heard another letter come through our mail slot. "It's for you, Pip," he said as he collected it.

I opened the unfamiliar envelope to discover that my sister had died. Even though she hadn't been too kind to me as a child, I was still angered by whoever hurt her. Mrs. Joe did see me safely through my childhood. And she had suffered so much since her accident. My heart ached to know she was gone and that Joe was now alone.

The morning of the funeral, I took a coach and made my way back to the Blue Boar hotel. Even though I had written to tell Joe I was coming, we hadn't spoken since that day in London. Guilt washed over me as I stowed my bags. I really should have come home more often to see my sister and Joe.

As I rounded the corner, I saw the funeral carriage outside the forge, with the procession about to begin. I walked up to Joe and put my hand on his shoulder. "Oh, Joe, how are you?"

He grabbed my hand and gave it a comforting squeeze. I knew then that everything was fine between us—that he had forgiven me for my terrible behavior.

"Pip, you knew her before the accident, when she was her right self. You know she meant the world to me. What will I do without her?"

We followed the carriage on foot. As the procession passed by the marshes, memories came to mind of that Christmas with my convict. Even though my sister had harsh ways, I still loved her. My entire family was gone—buried side by side in the church graveyard. I truly was an orphan. The thought was overwhelmingly sad.

After the funeral service, Biddy invited me to come home for a cold supper with her and Joe. I asked, "Would it be okay if I stayed in my old room tonight? I had booked a room in town, but it doesn't feel right . . ."

Joe smiled and said he'd be glad if I did. Once he went up to bed, I had a long talk with Biddy.

Biddy told me how my sister passed away, and that she was sad. Not only about my sister, but because she had nowhere to go now that Mrs. Joe had died. I said that Joe would need as much help as ever, and that she shouldn't worry.

"Did the police ever discover who hurt Mrs. Joe?" I asked.

"No," Biddy replied, "they never did. But we've suspected Orlick for some time. Not that it matters now."

Biddy said good night, and I climbed the stairs up to my little attic room. I looked out the window as I had done the night before I left for London. Home was no longer home. And I was different, too. I was no longer a scared little boy.

The next morning, after saying good-bye, I walked to catch my coach back to London. The familiar mists rose up from the marshes. What reason did I have to come back now?

CHAPTER 9

Pip Becomes a Gentleman

New clothes, fancy furniture, expensive dinners—Herbert and I lived well in London. Bills piled up unpaid. Allowances were quickly spent. We weren't bothered by our debts—we didn't even think about them. We were young and enjoyed our freedom. Like a true gentleman, I was well dressed, educated, and had no need to work.

On the day before my twenty-first birthday, a note arrived from Mr. Jaggers. Our meeting was scheduled for five o'clock the next afternoon.

Wemmick quietly wished me a happy birthday when I arrived, and then winked.

"Mr. Pip!" Mr. Jaggers called. "How do you feel now that you've come of age? Ready to start behaving?"

I hung my head with shame. Mr. Jaggers knew how foolish I had been with my allowance.

"Yes, sir," I said.

"You've been spending far too much money. You need to smarten up." He paused for a moment. "Do you understand?"

"I understand. Now that I'm of age will my benefactor be revealed?" I asked.

"Not yet," he said, "but here is your birthday present."

"It's a check for five hundred pounds!"

"This is all the money you will receive each year—enough with the careless spending." Mr. Jaggers looked me straight in the eye. "Do you remember the first time we met? I told you it could be a very long time until you knew the truth. We agreed—no questions."

I nodded. Mr. Jaggers said, "When the person chooses to be known, you won't need me any longer. That's all I'm going to say about it."

On Sunday I decided to go and visit Wemmick at his castle. I wanted to see if he could help me solve Herbert's and my money problems. The drawbridge was up, so I rang the bell. The elder Mr. Wemmick let me in. I was surprised he could hear the bell since he could hear little else.

"My son's gone for a walk with Miss Skiffins," he shouted. Miss Skiffins was Wemmick's lady friend. "He should be back soon."

The pair of us sat outside. Soon Wemmick came into sight and he waved from across the moat.

"Tally ho!" the aged parent yelled as he lowered the drawbridge. Miss Skiffins smiled, and Wemmick helped her across. She was young and sweet, even if she wore a dress that was a little too orange with gloves that were a little too green. Wemmick gave her a loving look.

"Pip," he said, "nice to see you! Shall we take a walk? Miss Skiffins will sit with dear aged parent."

As we walked, Wemmick showed me how different the castle grounds were now that it was winter. We were deep along the garden path when he finally said, "Now tell me what's bothering you?"

I said I didn't think it was fair that my future was so secure when Herbert would need to work hard to pay off his debts.

"Can I set aside some of my inheritance for him? Is there a way you can help me?" I asked.

Wemmick scratched his head. "Mighty good

of you to want to help Herbert. But I'm afraid there's nothing I can do."

"But you're a clerk!"

"I'm a *law* clerk," he said. "But Miss Skiffins's brother is an accountant. Maybe we can talk to him about creating a job for Herbert. You said he was interested in shipping?"

"Oh, yes, we spoke of it the first day we met."

"I'll bet Mr. Skiffins knows a business that would let you create a job for Herbert."

"I'd be willing to pay. I just don't want Herbert to know."

A few days passed before I got a note from Wemmick. The business had been taken care of. One of Mr. Skiffins's clients was a fairly new shipping merchant and didn't have enough money to run his business. He would take my hundred pounds a year and hire Herbert to help. One day, he said, he might even make Herbert a partner.

When the letter came about the new job, Herbert was so excited. He thought maybe Mr. Jaggers had set it up—he never knew I was involved. If only all of our money problems could be solved so easily.

Estella and I saw a lot of each other while she was only ten miles away in Richmond. We spent many summer afternoons picnicking, and I heard all about her life in high society. While walking one afternoon, she said, "Miss Havisham has called me home tomorrow. She insists that you take me."

I told her I'd hire a coach to take us. Estella was so important to me that I was happy to do anything she asked. After all, there had to be a reason why Miss Havisham had made me promise to be her friend. I decided she must want me to marry Estella. She had never said anything about it, of course. But why else would she help me to become a gentleman?

The coach dropped us off in front of Manor House the next day. The same dimly lit hallway led us to the same dreary room. Once we were seated inside, Miss Havisham couldn't stop talking about Estella's charm and her beauty. I thought, *Why is she talking like this? I already know everything about Estella, good and bad.*

Miss Havisham's eyes glowed as she talked about the glamorous parties Estella attended, about the important people she met. The quiet way Estella sat on the arm of Miss Havisham's chair made me finally realize something. She was using Estella!

The old worn wedding dress, the tattered flowers—Miss Havisham's happiness was lost the day she didn't get married. She had trained Estella to hurt people the way she had been hurt. And now she was sending her out among high society. It was mean, but I knew it was true. I could tell just from how they looked at each other. Everything Miss Havisham did was to mold Estella to be cold and cruel, despite her beauty.

The candle cast a strange light upon the room. The stopped clock, the decaying furniture, the unworn shoe. Estella and me. We were nothing but dolls to her. She had watched us play as children. Now she forced us to do the same as adults.

Estella stood up. Miss Havisham said meanly, "Don't you want to sit near me now? You have a cold heart!"

"I am what you've made me," Estella replied.

Neither spoke much from that point until we all went to bed. Tired but unable to sleep, I slipped out of my room. A ghost-like Miss

Havisham was wandering the hallway. I closed my bedroom door slowly and climbed back into bed. As I drifted off, I heard the eerie tapping of her cane and the awful sound of her crying.

CHAPTER 10

The Benefactor Revealed!

That strange night at Manor House haunted me for the next two years. I no longer went to school in Hammersmith, but I still shared an apartment with Herbert. I was alone one night reading when I heard heavy footsteps coming up the stairs.

Is it my sister's ghost? I shivered. Quickly getting hold of my senses, I opened the door. "Who's down there?"

A deep voice called, "I'm looking for Mr. Pip."

"I'm Pip. How can I help you? Is something the matter?"

A man passed under the stairway lamplight. When he reached the top of the stairs, I could tell he was very strong and had a long gray beard.

The man laughed, "You've grown up nicely since that day on the marsh."

I gasped. The man standing in front of me was my convict! Years might have passed, and we both might have changed—but as I looked closer, I realized I would know *that* face anywhere.

"You were kind to me," he said and held out his hands. I could do nothing but take them in my own. My convict grabbed them both tightly. "I haven't forgotten."

As he stepped forward to give me a hug, I said, "There's no need to thank me—if that's why you've come. As you can see—"

"See what?" he said.

"It's cold and rainy, so I can't ask you to leave.

But I see no reason for us to be friends."

He asked, "Will you at least offer me a drink?"

I nodded, and led the way into my apartment. As I poured the tea, I tried to keep my hand steady. For an instant, I felt like the little boy he'd tipped upside down in the graveyard.

Sitting down in a chair, he took a long sip. My voice shook slightly as I asked, "Do you work now?"

My convict replied, "I've had many jobs. Mainly I was a sheep farmer, far away from London."

"I hope you've been successful," I said.

"Very." He looked around the room at our fine furniture and asked, "How are you doing so well, Pip?" he asked.

I didn't know how to answer his question. His eyes twinkled as he said, "Don't you have a guardian named Mr. Jaggers?"

How does he know that? The room started to spin. "Been taken care of, too, by a clerk named Wemmick?"

I grasped the chair beside me so I wouldn't fall. He continued, "It's me, Pip! *I* am the one who made a gentleman of you. I've worked hard to give you everything!"

What? The convict was my benefactor? I shrank into the sofa cushions and looked at him with a mixture of confusion, fear, and hatred.

He went on, "I saw you every day in my mind just like that day on the marshes. I knew I wanted to help you in whatever way I could. I knew you'd do well. I knew it by the way you helped me all those years ago. I wanted to be like a father to you.

"Oh, I've looked forward to this day for so long. Did you ever guess it was me who gave you the fortune?"

"Oh, no," I whispered, barely able to speak. "Never."

My convict told me all about his new life. As he told me how he had made his fortune in Australia raising sheep, my stomach turned. My heart was crushed. My great expectations had *nothing* to do with Miss Havisham, nor Estella. They were all because of a convict! I felt sick.

The man then asked, "Where shall I sleep?"

"Pardon me?" I said.

"I've come all the way from Australia by ship. My journey was long and hard. If I don't get some rest I'll fall asleep in this chair." He laughed.

I sighed. "My roommate, Herbert, is away for a few days. You can stay in his room."

"No one will see me, right?" he said.

"What would it matter if you were seen?"

"They'll hang me this time if they catch me." He yawned. I couldn't believe he was still wanted by the law!

I showed my convict to Herbert's room and shuttered all the windows. Then I fell on my own bed in a miserable state. My world was in shambles. My benefactor had been and always would be a criminal. All my dreams—to fix Manor House for Miss Havisham and Estella—were dashed. But the worst part of it all? I had deserted good, kind Joe, and for nothing!

My landlady knocked the next morning asking how many for breakfast. I quickly lied, "Um, my uncle arrived late last night. Please prepare breakfast for two."

My convict came into the room and said good morning. "I don't even know your name," I said.

"When I came over on the ship, I was called Provis. You can call me that."

"It's not your real name?"

"My real name is Magwitch," he said. "Abel Magwitch."

"Did you see or talk to anyone last night before you came here?" I asked, worried someone might already know he was here.

"Not a soul," he replied.

Our breakfast arrived. Provis ate as if he had never seen food before. Every slurp, every spill reminded me of that morning on the marsh. I knew it was wrong, but I hated him.

"You look fine, Pip. It does me good to see you." He took a thick wallet out of his jacket and threw it on the table. "Everything in there is yours."

I couldn't pick it up. I didn't want *anything* from Provis.

"Enough!" I shouted. "Please stop talking about it—we have much bigger problems. What are your plans? How long are you staying here? How will you keep yourself safe?"

"No one but you, Mr. Jaggers, and Mr. Wemmick knows who I am. I'm not going back."

Provis laughed. "I'll need a disguise."

For the second time in my life, I acted in secret for my convict. I spent the day in town buying him new things and trying to find a place for him to stay. In the afternoon I went to see Mr. Jaggers.

He took one look at my troubled face and said, "I don't want to know anything . . ."

I sat down in an old leather chair. "He's told me everything."

"Don't you mean you've *heard* everything? You can't be *told* something by someone who is in Australia. As far as *I* know, he's been there since he was sent away on a prison ship years ago."

"Fine," I said. "I have *heard* that Abel Magwitch is my benefactor."

Mr. Jaggers nodded. "Yes, Abel Magwitch of *Australia.*"

I continued, "I always believed it was Miss Havisham."

Mr. Jaggers looked at me strangely. "Whatever gave you that idea? I suppose Mr. Provis has come to give you the good news?"

"Yes, that's the name he's using."

"Wonderful. I can send along the rest of your inheritance now. You're a very wealthy young man, Pip." He winked. "You should write to Magwitch in *Australia* to thank him."

CHAPTER 11

Herbert Knows Almost Everything

‿⁊

Herbert arrived home the next day. Before he had even taken off his hat, Provis came bounding forward with a tattered copy of the Bible. "Put your hand right there and swear." Herbert did as he was asked. "Now we can tell you the whole story!"

We spent many hours and two full meals listening to Provis's stories. Midnight came and went before he finally left for the room I had found for him down the road.

"I'm too stunned to think," Herbert said.

"I was, too, at first. He wants to spend all his money on me, carriages, and horses. He doesn't even want us to live at Barnard's Inn anymore—he thinks we should move to a better part of town."

"Will you accept the fortune?"

I said, "How can I? He's a criminal. But I am in debt and now in his debt. He's paid for everything these past few years." Herbert said, "You'll come and get a job with me." Poor Herbert had no idea it was Provis's money that had paid for his job in the first place.

"Plus, he's a very dangerous man. Remember the story he told us about the terrible fight he had with the other convict? How do you think he'd react if I just said *No, thanks, I don't want anything to do with you*?"

"I shudder to think of it." Herbert paced around the room for a moment. "I can only see one way out. We must get him out of England.

When he's away, you'll write and say you no longer want his help. It's the only way."

⌒

The next morning Provis arrived for breakfast, as usual. I asked, "Do you remember the night on the marshes long ago when you fought that other convict? You said you were helping the soldiers find and arrest him. Why was it so important to turn him in? It cost you your own freedom."

He said, "You're both still sworn to secrecy— Pip on your fortune, Herbert on my Bible." He stared at us through squinty eyes. "My life story is easy to tell. I was in jail. I was out of jail. That's about all there is to it. I don't know where I was born. I never had a proper home. I stole so I could eat, but I worked sometimes, too.

"I had a partner in crime for a long time. His name was Compeyson. He looked handsome and smart, like a real gentleman, but he was mean as a snake."

Provis warmed his hands by the fire. "He took me in and taught me things. But soon I couldn't get out from under his thumb. He had power over me, you see? I got sent to jail for stuff both of us had done.

"When I finally got out, I never should have gone back. But I did. When we were caught the next time, we were both sent to trial. Compeyson was well dressed and well spoken. He talked his way into mercy and seven years in jail. I got fourteen because of my ragged clothes and poor speech.

"I swore I'd get back at Compeyson for it. The night I found Pip, I had knocked him down as we both escaped from that prison ship.

"When Pip told me he saw another man on the marshes, I knew it was Compeyson and I had to catch him. I didn't care if I was in jail for

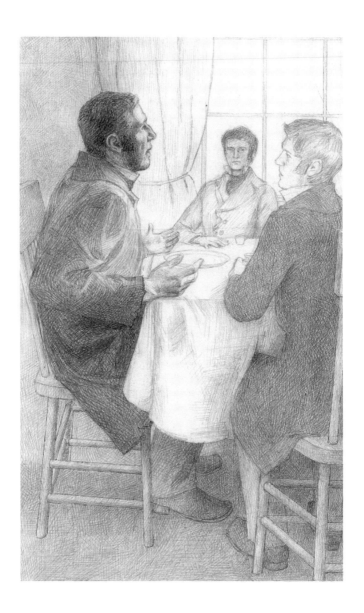

the rest of my life as long as he was there with me. No one, not the guards or the court, listened to my side before sending me away for life. I escaped again—as you can see, I'm sitting here in front of you—and made my fortune."

We were quiet for a moment until I asked, "Is Compeyson dead?"

"Maybe, maybe not. I haven't seen or heard of him since our last trial."

Herbert passed me a note under the table.

Compeyson is the name of the man who was to marry Miss Havisham!

I tried not to react as I tossed the note into the fire and looked at Herbert. "We have to get you out of London," I said to Provis, "before anyone knows you're here."

∽

Angry, confused, and unhappy, I knew I had to see Miss Havisham. I took the coach home the next morning hoping Estella would be there.

"What wind blows you here, Pip?" Miss Havisham said when she saw me. Sure enough, Estella was visiting at Manor House for the week. She put down her knitting when I walked in the room.

I cleared my throat. "Knowing who my benefactor is has made me terribly upset. I can't say more. It isn't my secret to tell."

Miss Havisham looked at me strangely, "What secret?"

I looked at her and then at Estella. "I never should have left Joe's forge. You were finished with me the day I became a blacksmith's apprentice."

"Indeed," Miss Havisham said.

"And Mr. Jaggers—" I started.

"Just a coincidence. He works for many people," she said.

"You led me to believe that you were the one paying for my education. That you were the one giving me great expectations."

Miss Havisham looked at me and said coldly, "I never led you to believe something that wasn't true, Pip."

Estella said nothing and went back to her knitting. I said, "I need your help. I have decided to give up the money. But I've been paying for Herbert's salary at his job up until now. I'm asking that you carry on for me now that I'll have no fortune."

They were both silent, but as the truth spilled out, I couldn't stop myself. "Miss Havisham, all this talk of me staying friends with Estella, of pushing us together—you never intended for us to marry, did you? It was just a game."

Miss Havisham did not reply. Estella looked up from her work. "I am engaged to Bentley Drummle."

"That brute!" I shouted. "I cannot believe you! I am breaking my promise, Miss Havisham. I'm afraid we aren't friends anymore, Estella."

Miss Havisham looked at me with blank eyes, showing no emotion.

"Pip," Miss Havisham said, "I have a note for Mr. Jaggers. Would you be so kind as to deliver it for me?"

I took the note from her cold hand and left Manor House without saying another word.

CHAPTER 12

The Escape Plan

حو

I was so upset that I walked all the way home to London. When I arrived at my front gate at Barnard's Inn, a man handed me a note.

Don't go home! Come and see me at the castle.

—Wemmick

The drawbridge was already down when I arrived. As I stepped across, Wemmick popped his head out the kitchen window and shouted, "You got my note!"

The aged parent served me a hot cup of tea.

Wemmick sat down at the table. "I heard a bad, bad fellow is looking for you. I'll not say his name, but I know he's looking for your 'uncle,' too," he whispered.

"Compeyson is alive and in London!" I shouted.

"Shhh," Wemmick said. "I've already talked to Herbert. Your 'uncle' is safely hidden away at a boardinghouse. Herbert's staying with him just to be sure."

Wemmick took out his pocket watch. "I've got to get to work. Stay here as long as you want, but be careful when you go see your 'uncle.'" He pressed a piece of paper with the address into my hand. "The last thing you need is that dangerous rascal finding any of you. There's no telling what he might do."

My feelings were still hurt from finding out how little Estella and Miss Havisham cared for me. I wasn't ready to see Provis and tell him the bad news about Compeyson. I needed to rest. I fell asleep by the fire in Wemmick's cozy living room and slept until much later that afternoon.

The boardinghouse was down by the docks. When I arrived, an elderly woman answered the door. She called for Herbert. He came downstairs and pulled me into the parlor.

Herbert whispered, "I haven't told Provis about Compeyson. He might rush off and do something crazy or get himself into more trouble."

"How did you get him to agree to hide?"

"I told him I thought someone might be watching us. He agreed right away."

"I've been to see Wemmick," I said. "We're not safe. Compeyson could be watching us. We'll need to stay apart for a while. But I still think we should stick to our original plan. How are we going to get Provis out of London?"

"I've got an idea," Herbert said. "We'll row him out of town. We can take him by boat to the Hamburg steamer. He should be safe enough in Germany."

We quickly discussed how it would work. In a few weeks' time, once things with Compeyson settled down, I'd row a rented boat down here to the boardinghouse. We'd sneak Provis out at night. When we told him, he seemed to like the plan. He agreed it would be safer for him to live somewhere other than London.

Herbert and I made regular trips out on the Thames River over the next few weeks. We rowed up and down so much that no one looked at us twice when we showed up, oars in hand.

Even though my arms grew strong, my heart remained broken. Estella was probably married to the awful Drummle by now. My days on the water were miserable. And my nights weren't much better. Trying to save some money, I ate poor food at awful places. Places like the playhouse where Mr. Wopsle was performing in yet another bad play.

One night, after the performance was finished, Wopsle caught me on the way out.

"Pip," he said, "how nice to see you. What happened to the other fellow?"

I spun my head around quickly. "What other fellow?"

"The one sitting behind you. He's been with you every night you've been here."

"What fellow?" I asked again.

"It's the strangest thing," Wopsle said. "Remember when you were a boy and those soldiers had captured those two convicts?"

"Yes, yes," I said.

"The fellow behind you looked just like the mean one."

The mean one! Compeyson! Compeyson had

been sitting behind me during the play night after night and I hadn't noticed. We would have to make our escape with Provis very soon.

∽

I saw Mr. Jaggers on my way to the river the next afternoon. He had a note for me from Miss Havisham.

"She'd like you to visit," Mr. Jaggers said, "as soon as possible."

Herbert and I decided I should go the next day. We planned Provis's escape from London for the day after that.

I didn't want to see Miss Havisham. What was left to say? Still, I hired a coach and was soon in the one place I thought I'd never be again.

The light must have played tricks on her eyes. She called out, "Pip, are you real?" when I stepped into the ballroom.

I answered, "Yes, Miss Havisham. Mr. Jaggers

gave me your note." I pulled a chair across the floor and sat down.

She said, "My heart isn't made of stone." She stretched out her old, bony hand and continued, "You said that something should be done about Herbert's salary?"

"I would like that very much," I said.

She asked, "How much money do you need?" I told her the exact amount. With a shaky hand, she wrote a note and addressed it to Mr. Jaggers.

She looked at me closely, "Is there nothing I can do for you, Pip? Nothing at all?"

"I would like to know the truth. The truth about who Estella's parents really are. The truth about your past. I want to know why you never told me about Compeyson." Miss Havisham began to shake and her eyes became glassy.

"I'm no longer angry with you," I said. "But you owe me an explanation. How have I come to be in the middle of all of this—how does Estella fit in? Why did you lie to us both?" She looked so old and worn that I felt bad for her. I said, "I have always loved Estella and always will, and that's your fault." I didn't even realize I loved Estella until I said it.

Miss Havisham whispered, her voice shaking, "I've done a terrible thing, haven't I? Brought you up to believe a fairy tale that never existed."

She said nothing further. I stood up and said, "Thank you for helping Herbert."

She cried softly as I left the room. Before leaving Manor House, I walked to the very spot in the garden where Herbert and I had once had that silly fight. All those years I looked for Estella's approval. All those years I thought that Miss Havisham was my benefactor. I looked at the overgrown weeds, the worn-down house.

The mist and the marshes were the same. But Miss Havisham and I were different. And I still didn't know the truth.

CHAPTER 13

The Getaway

The note from Miss Havisham gave me an excuse to go see Mr. Jaggers at his office the next morning. After he read it, he said, "I'm sorry that we can't do anything for you, Mr. Pip."

"It's enough to help Herbert. I don't want anything else but the truth. She couldn't even give that to me."

Mr. Jaggers bent forward and brushed some dirt off his boots, "What good would it do to learn the truth now, after all these years?" he said.

I replied that I had a right to know. It was more than just fate that tied Miss Havisham, Estella, and me together. I wanted Mr. Jaggers to fill in the pieces.

He sighed. "Do you remember meeting my housekeeper, Molly?" Mr. Jaggers then told me Provis had been married to Molly once, and they had a daughter. At the time, Provis was still working for Compeyson. Provis, Molly, and Compeyson made a terrible mistake. They tried to rob someone, and that person ended up dead. Molly was brought up on charges of murder. Mr. Jaggers defended her in the trial and won. She asked him to take the child away to safety. The girl, Estella, was given to Miss Havisham.

I jumped at the mention of Estella's name. She was Provis's daughter?

"Provis was sent away on the prison ship, and hasn't seen Molly or his daughter since. You see, Mr. Pip, I tried to keep them both safe. Provis was a great friend to me," Mr. Jaggers said. "We got to know each other well over the years. He was a good man stuck in a bad situation. I've never trusted that snake, Compeyson."

"Sir!" Wemmick shouted from the other room. "You're needed out here."

I stood up and shook Mr. Jaggers's hand. I thanked him for telling me the truth. I was shocked that Compeyson had ruined not only Provis's life, but Molly's and Estella's, too. It was strange to find out that all these relationships existed. I'd never known about them until now.

As daylight began to open up the sky, Herbert and I were already rowing hard along the Thames. Bundled in our coats, we were making the big escape today.

"We're in agreement, we'll row to the

Hamburg steamer?" Herbert said as softly as he could.

"I think we can make the early one, tomorrow morning. Don't you?" I replied.

Herbert said, "I still think it's best if you stay with Provis as long as you can—it will be safer. I can row the boat back to London and be back at work in two days' time."

We landed the boat at the docks near Provis's boardinghouse. "Is he where we told him to be?" I whispered to Herbert.

"Here he comes."

Provis slipped onto the boat, and we were quickly off. "Thank you, dear boys," he said.

"If all goes well, you'll be free and safe in a few days," I said.

We rowed all day and through the night. As careful as we thought we had been, we couldn't shake the feeling that we were being followed. We strained our eyes to see if there were other boats on the water. There were none we could see.

"Is anyone hungry?" Provis asked.

Herbert said, "I'm starving! Let row to shore and find something to eat."

"Good idea," I said. "I can see a light on over there. Perhaps it's an inn."

We pulled the boat up to where the light from the inn hit the shore. I took a quick look around and couldn't see any reason not to stop. The inn had warm food and soft beds, so we decided to stay for the night.

The next morning we were barely on the water before a fast-moving boat pulled up beside us. A man shouted, "You've got Abel Magwitch on board. He must surrender immediately!" It was Compeyson!

"You scoundrel!" Provis shouted. Compeyson reached over the side of his boat and grabbed Provis by the shoulders. Before Herbert or I could do anything, both men went overboard!

I couldn't even grab Provis's boots before he went underwater. I heard a loud crash and a cannonball landed in the middle of our boat. Compeyson had thrown it onboard! Within minutes, Herbert and I were in the water, our boat sunk.

Almost out of nowhere came a large navy steamer ship. Within minutes the soldiers had pulled Herbert and me out of the water. Compeyson's boat drifted farther and farther away. I couldn't see him or Provis.

"Over there!" Herbert shouted. I followed his finger to see Provis swimming fast toward us. The guards pulled him out of the water badly injured, but alive.

"We have a warrant for your arrest, Abel Magwitch," the sergeant said. "I have to put you back in cuffs. You boys are lucky you aren't in more trouble," he said before he left us alone.

"What happened to Compeyson?" I asked Magwitch.

"I took him overboard with me, and we fought, but he got away."

The navy ship went back to London. Magwitch had lost the wallet during his fight with Compeyson in the water. It was filled with his banknotes and property deeds. His entire fortune was lost! He was headed back to jail for certain. He must have seen the sorrow on my face.

"Don't be sad, Pip," he said. "None of this

matters now. I'm just happy to have seen you become a gentleman." He drifted off to sleep then, with Herbert and me by his side.

When we got back to London, Magwitch was taken straight to court. They sent him to jail until it came time for his trial.

The police searched for Compeyson. His body washed up to the shore three days later. In his pocket, they found a notebook. It was filled with plans about how he was going to steal everything from Magwitch. Even so, without the original documents that were in the wallet, Magwitch couldn't prove the fortune was his.

During the trial I tried to convince the courts that Compeyson was the true villain. I used myself as an example: a poor, common boy turned into a gentleman by a goodhearted man. Who cared if he had made some mistakes in his life? My arguments fell on deaf ears. He was found guilty. Once a criminal, always a criminal.

"Thank you, Pip," he said when I came to see him in prison after the trial. "You've never left my side."

"I wouldn't," I said. Magwitch's health had been poor since that night on the river. "Are you in much pain?"

"Nothing to complain about," he said. My feelings toward him were different now. I could see he was a good man, someone who tried to change. He gave up everything so I could have a better life. I decided he deserved the truth.

I took a deep breath and told him the story about how I'd discovered that Estella was his daughter. I told him Estella had grown up to be a beautiful woman. He smiled, squeezed my hand, and then he was gone.

"No!" I cried, trying to wake him. I wanted to thank him for all he had done for me. I wanted to tell him I thought he was a good person. But now I couldn't.

As I left for the last time, I bent down beside the walls of the prison with my head in my hands. Tears streamed down my face. We had both made mistakes. Magwitch had trusted Compeyson, and I had believed in Miss Havisham. We were both common men trying to better our lives. The only difference was that Magwitch gave me everything because I was once kind to him. That Christmas on the marsh had changed us both.

The next few days passed in a blur. I had no money to pay my debts and was in deep trouble. The events of the past few weeks—Magwitch's death, losing my fortune—took their toll. I fell into a terrible fever and didn't wake for many days. When I came around, I was happy to discover that Joe had been taking care of me.

"Joe," I whispered, "you've come."

"I have, Pip. I had to. You've been very sick. Biddy told me to come, and I did."

"Joe, thank you, thank you so much," I said.

He smiled. "Pip, I have such news for you."

Joe told me that Miss Havisham had passed away, too. There were so many changes back home that Joe could barely get them all out. Each day I grew stronger, and he stayed with me until I was almost well. But what was even more kind? Joe paid all my debts.

I decided it was time to go home. Three days later that's exactly what I did. I happily discovered that Biddy and Joe had gotten married.

After a few happy months at home, I decided to join Herbert, whose work had sent him far away—to Cairo, Egypt. The merchant he worked for had made him a partner, just as he said he would. Herbert's dream of owning a shipping empire had come true at last. We lived well. Even though I wasn't a gentleman, I had everything I wanted.

Eleven years had passed since the last time I went home to see Joe. But something called me back, and I knew I had to go. The three of us—Joe, Biddy, and I—shared a lovely dinner. They had a little boy they called Pip, and he was a sweet child. I laughed when I saw him sitting in my old corner. I had never seen either of them so happy.

After supper, I walked alone to Manor House to pay my respects. Neither the factory nor the house was still there. As the mist rose around the old courtyard, the place looked as strange as it had when I first saw it all those years ago as a young boy.

I opened the rusty old gate and walked through the garden. I noticed someone else was also there.

It can't be! I thought.

"Estella!" I shouted.

"Pip," she said. "I look so different, it's a wonder you even recognized me."

"How odd that we're both here at the very same moment. Do you come back often?"

She answered, "Never, this is the first time."

"For me, too," I said.

"The grounds belong to me now," she said. "Are you still living far away?"

"Yes," I said. "I do quite well."

"I think about you all the time," she said. I told her that I thought about her, too. She asked if I could ever forgive her for being so mean all those years ago. Of course I forgave her. I realized our lives were forever meant to be linked. We walked together, away from Manor House, hand in hand.

What Do *You* Think?
Questions for Discussion
⌒

Have you ever been around a toddler who keeps asking the question "Why?" Does your teacher call on you in class with questions from your homework? Do your parents ask you questions about your day at the dinner table? We are always surrounded by questions that need a specific response. But is it possible to have a question with no right answer?

The following questions are about the book you just read. But this is not a quiz! They are designed to help you look at the people, places, and events in the story from different angles. These questions do not have specific answers. Instead, they might make you think of the story in a completely new way.

Think carefully about each question and enjoy discovering more about this classic story.

1. When Pip first comes across Magwitch in the churchyard, the convict threatens to hurt him if he doesn't bring him a file and food. Why do you think Pip doesn't simply tell his sister and Joe what happened instead of stealing the food from the pantry? What would you have done in Pip's situation?

2. What is the relationship between Joe and Pip? Do you think they are more like family or more like friends? Do you have any friends who you consider to be like family? Any family members you consider to be good friends?

3. Why do you think Estella treats Pip the

way she does when they first met? Does her behavior toward him change by the end of the story? Have you ever made friends with someone you didn't like at first?

4. Why do you think Miss Havisham requests Pip's company at Manor House? Do you think you would have enjoyed spending time there? Would you and Miss Havisham have gotten along well?

5. When Mr. Jaggers tells Pip that he has come into money, Pip's life suddenly changes. He plans to move to London to become a gentleman. Do you think he has a choice about this? If you were given the choice, would you have stayed at home with Joe or gone to London?

6. Herbert and Pip become friends right away, even though they had that fight at Manor House years ago. Do you think the roommates have a strong friendship? Do you have any friends with whom you would like to live?

7. In the book, Pip becomes a "gentleman." What is your definition of a true gentleman? Does Pip live up to that definition?

8. When Magwitch comes to Pip in London, he calls himself Provis. Why do you think he changes his name? Have you ever wanted to change your name? Why?

9. Why do you suppose Miss Havisham asks Pip to promise her he'd always remain Estella's friend? Would you have promised Miss Havisham the same?

10. When Estella and Pip meet again in the last scene at Manor House, how do they seem to feel about each other? What do you think happens with them after the story ends?

A Note to Parents and Educators

By Arthur Pober, EdD

⌒⌒

First impressions are important.

Whether we are meeting new people, going to new places, or picking up a book unknown to us, first impressions count for a lot. They can lead to warm, lasting memories or can make us shy away from any future encounters.

Can you recall your own first impressions and earliest memories of reading the classics?

Do you remember wading through pages and pages of text to prepare for an exam? Or were you the child who hid under the blanket to read with a flashlight, joining forces with Robin Hood to save Maid Marian? Do you remember only how long it took you to read a lengthy novel such as *Little Women*? Or did you become best friends with the March sisters?

Even for a gifted young reader, getting through long chapters with dense language can easily become overwhelming and can obscure the richness of the story and its characters. Reading an abridged, newly crafted version of a classic novel can be the gentle introduction a child needs to explore the characters and story-line without the frustration of difficult vocabulary and complex themes.

Reading an abridged version of a classic novel gives the young reader a sense of independence and the satisfaction of finishing a "grown-up" book. And when a child is engaged with and inspired by a classic story, the tone is set for further exploration of the story's themes, characters, history, and details. As a child's reading skills advance, the desire to tackle the original, unabridged version of the story will naturally emerge.

If made accessible to young readers, these stories can become invaluable tools for understanding themselves in the context of their families and social environments. This is why the Classic Starts series includes questions that stimulate discussion regarding the impact and social relevance of the characters and stories today. These questions can foster lively conversations between children and their parents or teachers. When we look at the issues, values, and standards of past times in terms of how we live now, we can appreciate literature's classic tales in a very personal and engaging way.

Share your love of reading the classics with a young child, and introduce an imaginary world real enough to last a lifetime.

Dr. Arthur Pober, EdD

Dr. Arthur Pober has spent more than twenty years in the fields of early childhood and gifted education. He is the former principal of one of the world's oldest laboratory schools for gifted youngsters, Hunter College Elementary School, and former Director of Magnet Schools for the Gifted and Talented for more than 25,000 youngsters in New York City.

Dr. Pober is a recognized authority in the areas of media and child protection and is currently the U.S. representative to the European Institute for the Media and European Advertising Standards Alliance.

Explore these wonderful stories in our
Classic Starts™ library.